The Adventures of The Little Red Train

Benedict Blathwayt

RED FOX

THE ADVENTURES OF THE LITTLE RED TRAIN
A RED FOX BOOK 0 09 945693 1

The Runaway Train first published by Julia MacRae in 1995
Little Red Train to the Rescue first published by Julia MacRae in 1997
Faster, Faster, Little Red Train first published by Julia MacRae in 1999

This Red Fox edition published 2004

1 3 5 7 9 10 8 6 4 2

Red Fox Books are published by Random House Children's Books,
61–63 Uxbridge Road, London W5 5SA,
a division of The Random House Group Ltd,
in Australia by Random House Australia (Pty) Ltd,
20 Alfred Street, Milsons Point, Sydney, NSW 2061, Australia,
in New Zealand by Random House New Zealand Ltd,
18 Poland Road, Glenfield, Auckland 10, New Zealand,
and in South Africa by Random House (Pty) Ltd,
Endulini, 5A Jubilee Road, Parktown 2193, South Africa

THE RANDOM HOUSE GROUP Limited Reg. No. 954009
www.**kids**at**randomhouse**.co.uk

A CIP catalogue record for this book is available from the British Library.

Printed in Singapore

THE RUNAWAY TRAIN

Duffy Driver overslept.
Everyone was waiting at the
station for the little red train.

VISIT
PORLOCK

When Duffy was ready to start, he saw an old lady running down the platform. "I'll help you," he said. But he forgot to put the brake on and the little red train set off down the track . . .
Chuff-chuff, chuff-chuff, whoo . . . oooo

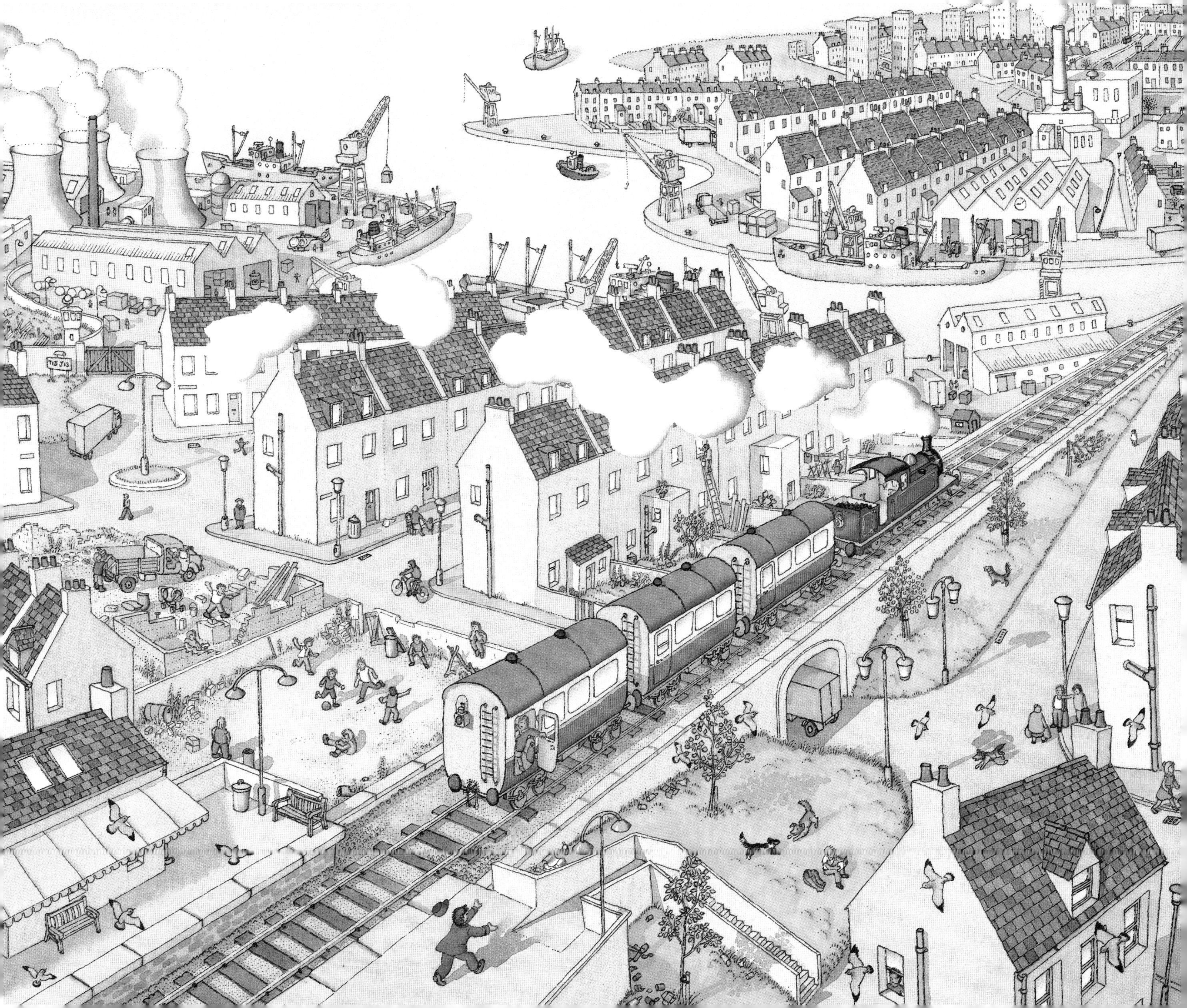
T15 J13

Duffy saw a lorry. “Stop!” Duffy shouted. “I must catch up with the runaway train!”

“Jump in,” cried the lorry driver and off they went after the little red train . . . *Chuff-chuff, chuff-chuff, whoo . . . oooo . . .*

. . . until they came to a traffic jam.

Duffy saw a boat. "Ahoy there!" Duffy shouted. "I must catch up with the runaway train!"

"All aboard," cried the boatman and off they all went after the little red train . . . *Chuff-chuff, chuff-chuff, whoo . . . oooo . . .*

. . . until the river turned away from the railway.

Duffy saw some bicycles. "Help!" Duffy shouted. "I must catch up with the runaway train!"

"Jump on," cried the cyclists and off they all went after the little red train . . . *Chuff-chuff, chuff-chuff, whoo . . . oooo . . .*

. . . until they ran into a flock of sheep.

Duffy saw some ponies. "Whoa!" Duffy shouted. "I must catch up with the runaway train!"
"Up you come," cried the riders and off they all went after the little red train . . . *Chuff-chuff, chuff-chuff, whoo . . . oooo . . .*

. . . until the ponies could go no further.

Duffy saw a tractor. "Halloo!" Duffy shouted. "I must catch up with the runaway train!"
"Get on then," cried the farmer and off they went after the little red train . . . *Chuff-chuff, chuff-chuff, whoo . . . oooo . . .*

. . . until they were spotted by a helicopter pilot.

"My last chance!" gasped Duffy. "I must catch up with the runaway train!"
"Climb in quick," said the pilot and Duffy climbed in, while the lorry driver, the boatman, the cyclists, the riders and the farmer all stood and watched . . .

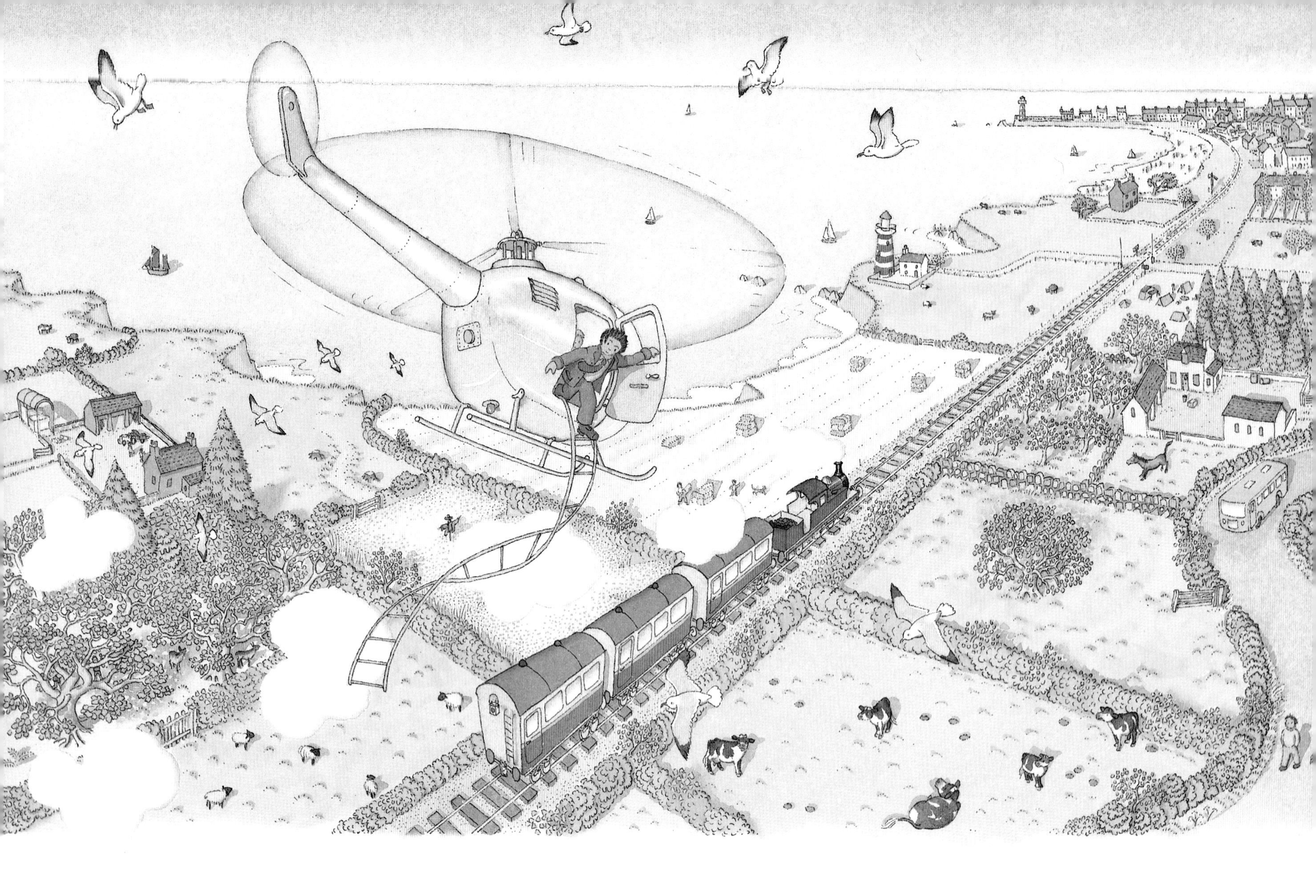

as Duffy caught up with the runaway train . . . *Chuff-chuff, chuffitty-chuff, whoo . . . oo . . . oo*

And Duffy Driver drove the little red train into the station at Sandy-on-Sea and spent a lovely lazy afternoon on the beach before he had to drive back home again.

Chuff-chuff, chuffitty -chuff, whoo . . . eee . . . eee . . .

LITTLE RED TRAIN TO THE RESCUE

One wet and windy day, Duffy Driver lit the fire in the little red train and collected three trucks from the goods yard.

The trucks were soon loaded and Duffy Driver and the little red train set off for Birchcombe village, high up in the hills. Chuff-chuff,chuffitty-chuff...

But as they came round a bend, what did they see...

Animals on the line!
Duffy put on the brakes with a scree...eee...ch
and the little red train stopped just in time.

When the animals were back in the
farmyard, the little red train set off again.
Chuff-chuff, chuffitty-chuff...

But as they came round a bend, what did they see...

The river had flooded the road!
Duffy put on the brakes with a scree...eee...ch
and the little red train stopped just in time.

They rescued the passengers from the bus on
the bridge and the little red train set off again.
Chuff-chuff, chuffitty-chuff...
But as they came round a bend, what did they see...

The wind had blown down a tree!
Duffy put on the brakes with a scree...eee...ch
and the little red train stopped just in time.

Everyone helped to move the tree
and the little red train set off again.
Chuff-chuff, chuffitty-chuff...

But the track got steeper and steeper and
the little red train hotter and hotter until...

P O P! HISSSSS! The safety valve blew off the boiler! Duffy Driver put on the brakes with a scree...eee...ch and stopped to let the little red train cool down.

Up in the hills there was snow,
so they set off again more slowly.
Chuff-chuff-chuff, chuu...ff, chuff...itty-chu...ff...
But as they came round a bend, what did they see...

A great pile of snow was blocking the line!
Duffy put on the brakes with a scree...eee...ch
and the little red train stopped just in time.

They all helped to clear the snow
and the little red train set off again.
Chuff-chuff, chuffitty-chuff...

But as they came to the last stretch
of line what did they find...

The points had frozen!
The little red train went off the wrong way.
Duffy put on the brakes with a scree...eee...ch
and the little red train stopped just in time.

The signalman poured hot water on the points and with a chuff-chuff, chuffitty-chuff the little red train ran on towards the station at Birchcombe...

POST OFFICE
BIRCHCOMBE
STORES

Everyone was there to greet them.
Duffy Driver blew the whistle, whee...eee...eee
and put on the brakes with a scree...eee...ch and the
little red train stopped at the platform just in time.

The passengers climbed down and helped to unload the supplies...

and Duffy Driver was given a special tea by the postmistress.

Then Duffy got back into the driver's cab and after he had blown the whistle, whee...eee...eee, the little red train raced back home. It was downhill all the way.

OFFICE

Chuffitty-chuffitty,
chuffitty-chuff...

Faster, Faster, Little Red Train

Duffy Driver was eating his breakfast when the telephone rang. "The fast train to Pebblecombe has broken down," he said. "The Little Red Train is needed. I'll have to rush."

The passengers from the broken-down train were cross and worried. "Will the Little Red Train get there on time, we don't want to miss the fair!"
"All aboard for Pebblecombe," called Duffy Driver.
"We'll go as fast as we can!"
Chuff chuff went the Little Red Train.
Click clack went the wheels on the track.

Their first stop was Newtown.
"Who's for Pebblecombe fair?" shouted Duffy Driver.
"Quick as you can!"
A lady with a big box of strawberries climbed on board.
Whoosh went the steam from the Little Red Train.
Click clack went the wheels on the track.
Click clack clicketty clack.

Next they stopped at Woodhaven.
"Jump on for Pebblecombe fair!" shouted Duffy Driver.
A man with a crate of hens squeezed into the carriage.
"You're running late," he grumbled.
"We're doing our best," Duffy Driver said cheerfully.
Chuff chuff went the Little Red Train.
Click clack went the wheels on the track.
Click clack clicketty clack.

The Little Red Train stopped at Castle Down.
"We're in a hurry," said Duffy Driver, "this train's for Pebblecombe fair."
A gang of noisy children climbed on board.
Chuff chuff went the Little Red Train.
Chuff chuff, chuffitty chuff...

The next station was Old Harbour.

"Any passengers for Pebblecombe?" called Duffy Driver.

"Is this the right train?" said a boy with a great big dog.

"It is the right train," said Duffy. "And we've no time to lose."

Whoo...eee... whistled the Little Red Train.

Chuff chuff chuffitty chuff.

When they stopped at Hillside station, there were four musicians waiting on the platform.

"We're playing at Pebblecombe fair," they grumbled, "and we're going to be late."

"In you get," said Duffy briskly, "we're going as fast as we can."

Whoo...eee... went the Little Red Train. *Whoo...eeee...*

The Little Red Train went faster than ever before.
Click clack went the wheels on the track.
Clicketty clicketty clicketty clack.
"Slow down," said the lady with the strawberries.

"Slow down!" shouted the man with the crate of hens.
"Slow down!" shrieked the boy with the great big dog.
"Steady on!" cried the musicians.
"Faster ... faster!" yelled the noisy children.

But Duffy Driver couldn't hear anyone shouting.
He shovelled more coal into the firebox and
the boiler made more and more steam and
the wheels of the Little Red Train went
faster and faster and faster...
Clicketty clicketty clicketty clicketty clicketty clicketty clack.

And right on time the Little Red Train
pulled into the station at Pebblecombe.

Out got the lady with her box of strawberries, the man with the hens and the boy with the dog and the four musicians and the gang of noisy children.

They thanked Duffy Driver and the Little Red Train for getting them to Pebblecombe so fast. Then they all went off to spend the day at the fair.

Duffy Driver thought he would have another breakfast.
"You're the Little Red Express now," he said as he wiped down the fenders.
*Whoo…eeee…*went the Little Red Train.
Whoo…oooo…eeee…